Jake Bakes a
MONSTER CAKE

LUCY ROWLAND MARK CHAMBERS

MACMILLAN CHILDREN'S BOOKS

One Saturday, Jake decided to bake
A cake for his friend's birthday tea.

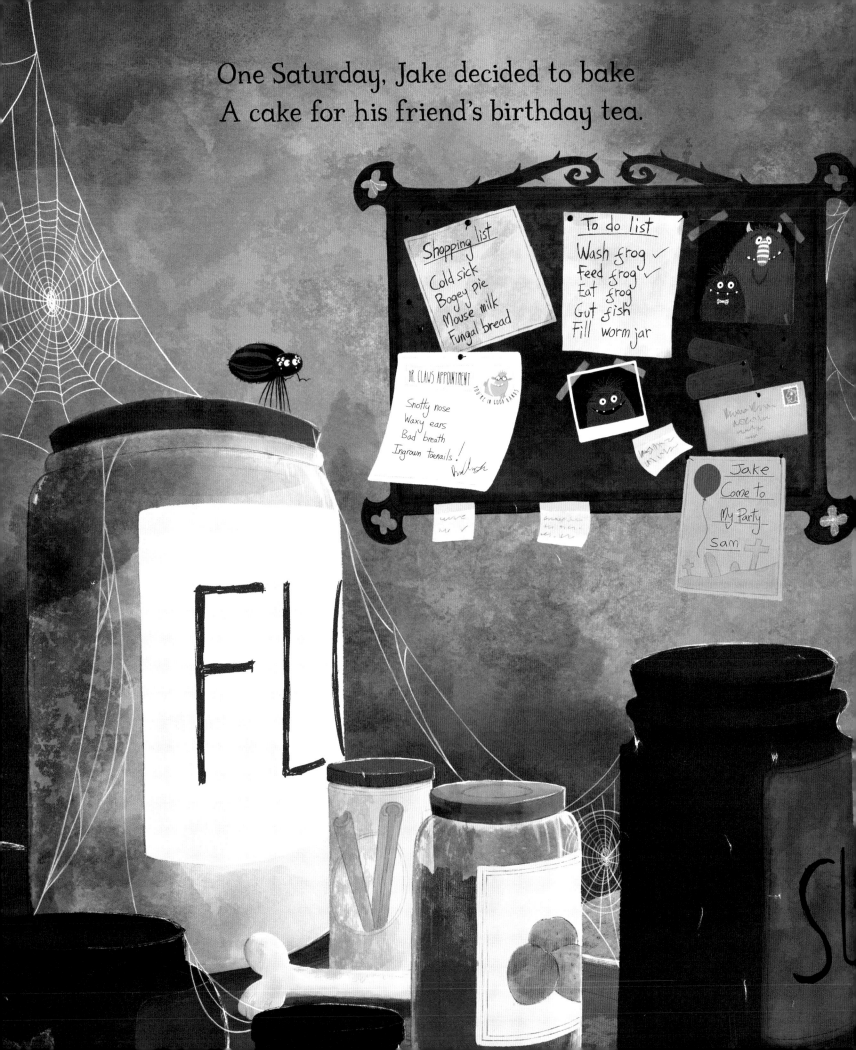

October

The DAILY FANG

GRRR! NO WE SAY NO!

MONSTERS STRIKE! OVER GREAT CAKE-OFF NEWS

He said, "What a treat!
Sam *loves* something sweet,
And my friends can help make it with me."

But you see it was tricky, Jake's friends were so picky,
Their plans were quite different to Jake's.

They liked juicy bugs
And fat slimy slugs
To flavour their favourite cakes.

That day Monster Tor arrived at Jake's door
And Ben walked behind with young Fred.

Tilly was late
But she rushed through the gate.
"It's time to get started," Jake said.

They hurried inside, and with aprons all tied,
Jake showed them the recipe book.

But Tor laughed with Tilly,
"Oh Jake, don't be silly!
We don't need *instructions* to cook!"

She grabbed smelly eggs,
   eight spidery legs,
Five ants, some old pants -
   about ten.

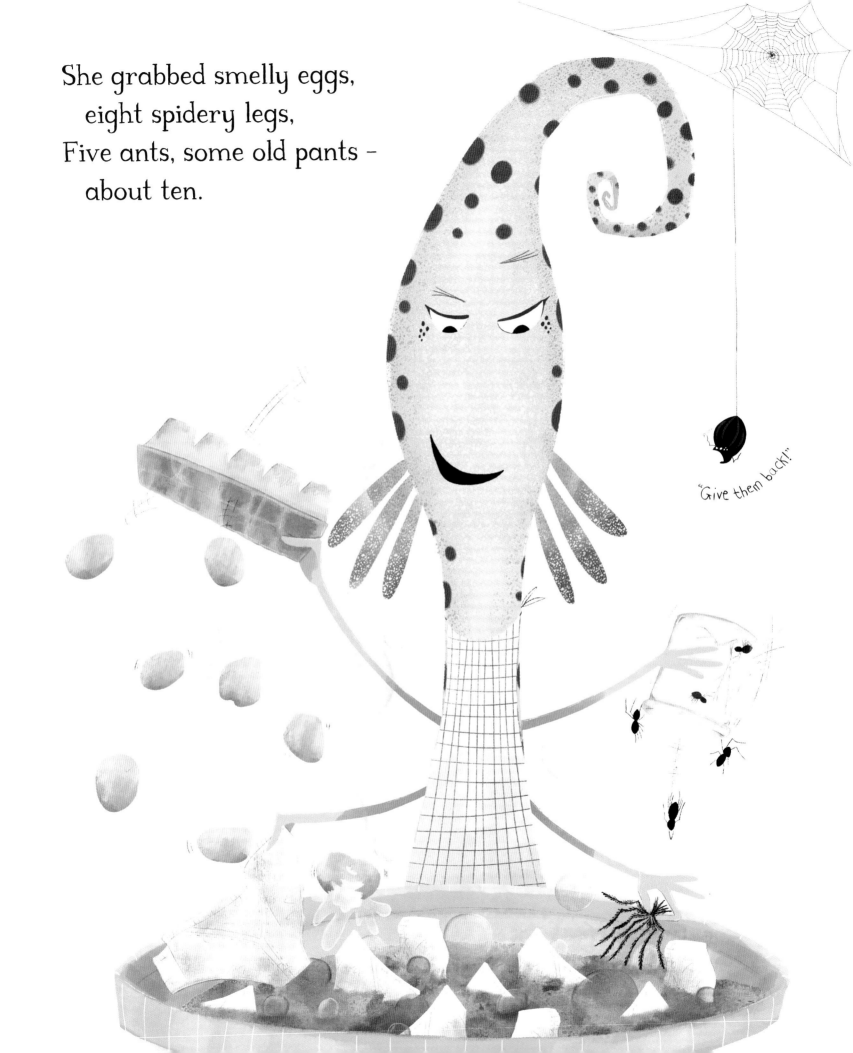

"Give them back!"

She whisked them
and whirred them,

She mixed them
and stirred them,

Then handed the
bowl on to Ben.

Ben shouted, "My turn!" And he threw in a worm.
He laughed, "It says here to add LIME!

Oh, do me a favour!
No, my kind of flavour
Is luminous bogey-green SLIME!"

Jake started to mutter, "But what about butter? Perhaps some more sugar?" he tried.

Fred thought for a minute,
Then threw a SLUG in it.
"But these are so gooey!" he cried.

Tilly said, "Please can I add in some cheese?
I promise it's really delicious!

It's stinky and old,
It's covered in mould . . .

And the maggots are extra nutritious!"

But Jake said, "Enough! Now, I'll have to get tough.
You'll ruin our present for Sam!"

Then a splash of the paste
Landed right on Jake's face . . .

"YUM!
What a good
baker I am!"

With the mixture cooked through,
Jake called the whole crew
To carry the *huge* bake outside.

SAM'S
HOUSE

But then in a muddle,
Jake slipped in a puddle . . .

"Uh-oh!"

And groaned as he watched the cake slide!

Sam opened his door as the cake hit the floor.
It fell with a SPLAT to the ground.

"Happy birthday," sobbed Jake,
While Sam stared at the cake,
And nobody else made a sound.

"I'm sorry," Jake cried,
his eyes open wide,
Sam frowned and he
puffed out his chest.

He turned towards Jake,
"When it comes to good cake . . .